Minnesota

Wisconsin

Michigan

New Hampshire

Vermont

New York

Iowa

Illinois

Indiana

Ohio

Pennsylvania

Massachusetts

Rhode Island

Connecticut

New Jersey

Nebraska

West Virginia

Virginia

Delaware

Maryland

Washington D.C.

Kansas

Missouri

Kentucky

North Carolina

Oklahoma

Arkansas

Tennessee

South Carolina

Alabama

Georgia

Texas

Mississippi

Louisiana

Florida

The Twelve Days of Christmas in Wisconsin

Erin Eitter Kono

Dear Adeline,
Merry Christmas!
We love you!
Andrew + Kelly
2008

STERLING
New York / London

Dear Emma,

Merry Christmas from Wisconsin! I can't believe you're coming to visit so soon! You'll want to know all that's great about my favorite state before you come to see it, right? We've got hills and forests and rivers and lakes, and some big cities full of stuff to do and see. I could never tell you everything there is to know in one short letter. So every day for the next twelve days, I'll be sending you just a little bit of our state. Hope you have a big closet. Get ready!

Your cousin, Jake

P.S. Wisconsin winters are REALLY cold. Pack your hat and mittens. Scarf and snowsuit. Ski goggles, thermal underwear, earmuffs, woolly socks, snowshoes....

Dear Emma,

Say hello to Earl the robin, my best feathered friend. If you give him lots of juicy worms, he'll perch on your shoulder and sing. His favorite tune is our state song, "On, Wisconsin!"

In 1927, Wisconsin kids got together and picked the robin as our state bird. Winters in the northern part of the state are much too cold for robins, so Earl usually flies south for the holidays. He was excited to visit you instead, but wouldn't leave home without our state tree, the sugar maple, so I'm sending you one. Every fall its leaves turn as red as Earl's chest, and every spring we tap the tree's sap to make maple syrup. When you get here, we'll pour some on Mom's fluffy pancakes. Yum!

Jake

On the first day of Christmas,
my cousin sent to me...

a robin in a
sugar maple
tree.

Dear Emma,

Dad drives a minivan, but when I grow up, I'm going to drive a Duck! It's a car and a boat all in one. During World War II, Ducks were used by brave soldiers to land on beaches and cross rivers. After the war, one of those soldiers realized that Ducks are perfect for exploring the Dells of the Wisconsin River. Every summer we take a Duck tour of the Dells, starting in the woods and then splashing into the river. From the water we see twisting, narrow gorges and look up at huge sandstone cliffs, all formed during the last ice age. Lots of rare plants and animals live in the Dells, but my favorite is a little fern called maidenhair spleenwort (also a good name for little sisters).

Don't forget to bring your swimsuit. The Dells area is famous for being the year-round water park capital of the world!

Jake

On the second day of Christmas, my cousin sent to me...

2 roving Ducks

and a robin in a sugar maple tree.

Dear Emma,

Larry, Curly, and Moe, my three pet lake sturgeon, were very jealous when Earl and the two Ducks left to meet you. They moped and refused to come up from the bottom of Lake Winnebago when I whistled! So I'm sending them to you. I think you'll agree that they are really cool fish.

Lake sturgeon can live to be over 150 years old and grow to be huge: one was measured at 7 ½ feet long and 310 pounds! Can you believe that sturgeon have been around since the time of the dinosaurs? Modern life isn't so easy for them, though—water and air pollution can make them really sick, and people sometimes take too many of their eggs to make a fancy snack called caviar. There were fewer and fewer sturgeon splashing around in Wisconsin's waters each year until fish lovers fought for laws to protect them. Now they are making a comeback!

Jake

On the third day of Christmas, my cousin sent to me...

3 huge fish

2 roving Ducks,
and a robin in a sugar maple tree.

Dear Emma,

My dog Bessie just had puppies! Meet Willie, Winnie, Walt, and Whip. You'd better learn to speak Puppy. Here are the basics:

Crazy kisses on your nose and ears early in the morning mean: "Wake up! Time for breakfast! HOORAY!" Front paws on the floor and tails in the air mean: "Oh, boy! Time to play! HOORAY!" When they get a little older they will want to run, fetch, and swim. That's because they are American Water Spaniels, a breed specially developed to help hunters track down ducks and geese in Wisconsin's river valleys. The American Water Spaniel is the only dog breed native to Wisconsin, and it is also our official state dog. These pups are easy to train, which means you can teach them to do great tricks! I'm training Bessie to howl "Rudolph the Red-Nosed Reindeer." She and Earl will do a fantastic duet.

Jake

On the fourth day of Christmas, my cousin sent to me...

4 pouncing pups

3 huge fish, 2 roving Ducks,
and a robin in a sugar maple tree.

Dear Emma,

Want to go to the circus with me? Good! We'll pack our bags for Baraboo, Wisconsin, home of the Circus World Museum. Every summer, circus performers in Baraboo put on shows and teach visitors about circus history. You can see crazy clown acts, listen to silly circus musicals, and even learn about Wild West shows and circus history at the special library there. The circus jugglers, acrobats, and daredevils are guaranteed to knock you off your trapeze.

Since circus business in Baraboo is slow over the holidays, I convinced a few of the big-top performers to bring their act to you. The ringmaster is bringing his five golden rings and some big cats that were ready for a vacation. Maybe you'll learn how to juggle bananas or walk on stilts. Have fun!

Jake

On the fifth day of Christmas, my cousin sent to me...

5 golden rings

4 pouncing pups, 3 huge fish, 2 roving Ducks, and a robin in a sugar maple tree.

Dear Emma,

Wisconsin is not the biggest state, but it IS the birthplace of some really, really big things. A company in Sparta, Wisconsin, makes humongous statues that are found on roadsides all across America. They've made a fiberglass Paul Bunyan, Babe the Blue Ox, buffalo, pennies, dinosaurs, killer bees, and many other super sculptures.

My favorite giants are still here in Wisconsin. A colossal Trojan horse stands guard in the Dells. This famous wooden structure is big enough to have a go-kart track running right through it. And when you come to visit, we'll take a trip to the biggest fiberglass structure in the world, a giant fish outside the Freshwater Fishing Hall of Fame in Hayward, Wisconsin. This monster is 4 1/2 stories high and half a city block long! You can climb up to the observation deck built right into the fish's toothy mouth . . . if you dare. Chomp!

Jake

On the sixth day of Christmas, my cousin sent to me...

6 roadside giants

5 golden rings, 4 pouncing pups, 3 huge fish, 2 roving Ducks, and a robin in a sugar maple tree.

Emma, this is air traffic control. Ready for take-off in four . . . three . . . Oh, by the way, congratulations! You'll be my copilot while you're here! The famous air show in Oshkosh, Wisconsin, is coming up at the end of July, and I have to get ready. I'm sending you seven planes so that you and your friends can practice flying. You'll love it!

While you're here, we might get to see professional stunt pilots swirl high in the sky as they rehearse their moves for the aerobatics show. We'll check out strange-looking planes of the future and peek inside cool old ones, too, like the warbirds. The combat pilots who flew the planes are around sometimes. If we're lucky, they might climb into the old birds, rise into the sky, and zoom right over our heads. It sounds like really loud thunder!

. . . two . . . one . . . blast off!

Jake

On the seventh day of Christmas, my cousin sent to me...

7 planes a-swooping

6 roadside giants,
5 golden rings, 4 pouncing pups, 3 huge fish, 2 roving Ducks,
and a robin in a sugar maple tree.

Dear Emma,

Whoops! Some of our Wisconsin whooping cranes insisted on following your new planes. Whoopers are amazing and very rare birds. They were almost extinct when some smart scientists with a crazy idea came to the rescue. Baby cranes had no adults to teach them how to migrate south, so the scientists dressed up in white suits and pretended to be mama birds. Then they taught the chicks to follow them in ultralight planes all the way from Wisconsin to Florida! Now those cranes are teaching their own chicks to migrate.

With lots of state parks and giant lakes, Wisconsin is a great place to visit if you like nature. If we go for a hike, maybe we'll see some bald eagles, elk, or even a coyote. Aroooo!

Did you know that Earth Day started here? Now, people around the country do good things for the planet every April 22, like planting trees, organizing recycling programs, and reminding politicians to protect our home. The whoopers are grateful!

Jake

On the eighth day of Christmas, my cousin sent to me...

8 cranes a-whooping

7 planes a-swooping, 6 roadside giants,
5 golden rings, 4 pouncing pups, 3 huge fish, 2 roving Ducks,
and a robin in a sugar maple tree.

Dear Emma,

Strap on your helmet and hold on tight—it's time for the World Championship Snowmobile Derby! Racers from all over the world gather in Eagle River, Wisconsin, to compete. The professionals, who go as fast as 100 miles an hour, say the trick to winning is not falling off!

Snow and ice have always been important in Wisconsin. Our state was even formed by icy glaciers. When Grandpa was a kid, before people had freezers, Wisconsin's frozen lakes were cut into chunks and delivered to family iceboxes to keep their food cold. Winter here is all about playing in the snow and even _with_ the snow. At the Flake Out Festival, you'll see amazing works of art at the official snow-sculpting competition. Then we'll head to Wausau for the Badger State Winter Games, the largest winter sports festival in the United States. We can watch the figure skaters, hang with the snowboarders, and play with the hockey team. Whoosh!

Jake

On the ninth day of Christmas, my cousin sent to me...

9 snowmobilers

8 cranes a-whooping, 7 planes a-swooping, 6 roadside giants,
5 golden rings, 4 pouncing pups, 3 huge fish, 2 roving Ducks,
and a robin in a sugar maple tree.

Dear Emma,

Shhhh, don't wake up the badgers! They may be cute, but these little guys can be fierce fighters—you don't want to be the one to make 'em mad. Badgers are shy, but they're proud Wisconsinites, too. When they heard that Earl was making the trip, our local badgers got together and insisted on meeting you.

The badger is the state animal of Wisconsin. Actually, people from this part of the country were called Badgers even before Wisconsin was a state! You see, badgers live in dens dug into the ground, where they keep cozy and warm all winter long. Some of Wisconsin's early settlers were tough lead miners, who decided to skip the trouble of building houses. Instead, they stayed warm by living in dens burrowed into the hillsides . . . just like badgers! Ever since, we've been called Badgers, and lots of Wisconsin teams use the fighting badger as a mascot, so . . . Go, Badgers!

Jake

On the tenth day of Christmas, my cousin sent to me...

10 badgers snoozing

9 snowmobilers,
8 cranes a-whooping, 7 planes a-swooping, 6 roadside giants,
5 golden rings, 4 pouncing pups, 3 huge fish, 2 roving Ducks,
and a robin in a sugar maple tree.

Dear Emma,

Who invented the ice cream sundae? Some people say that the idea of pouring syrup over ice cream was born in Two Rivers, Wisconsin. While the birthplace of the sundae is a huge debate, there are two things I know for sure:

1) It is better to eat a sundae (or eleven of them) than to talk about one.

2) Wisconsin takes ice cream, along with cheese, butter, and yogurt, very seriously. After all, we're America's Dairyland, producing more cheese than any other state. Each morning we have more cows to be milked than kids going to school! Wisconsin moms in the 1800s began making cheese so that extra milk wouldn't go to waste. Today, our cheeses—more than 600 kinds!—are eaten all over the world. In Monroe, Wisconsin, the Swiss Cheese Capital of the World, a Cheese Days Festival includes a big parade and a cow milking contest.

Ready . . . set . . . milk!

Jake

On the eleventh day of Christmas,
my cousin sent to me...

11
sundaes
melting

10 badgers snoozing, 9 snowmobilers,
8 cranes a-whooping, 7 planes a-swooping, 6 roadside giants,
5 golden rings, 4 pouncing pups, 3 huge fish, 2 roving Ducks,
and a robin in a sugar maple tree.

BOOZHOO, Emma!

Welcome to my birch bark bonanza! I learned to make birch bark baskets at camp. These baskets have been made in Wisconsin for hundreds of years by Native Americans, and were once used to gather foods like maple sap and wild rice. Tribes even turned the watertight containers into cooking pots. Natives of Wisconsin also used birch bark to make fast, lightweight canoes, cradleboards for carrying babies, and warm wigwams for homes. Today, more Native American tribes still live in Wisconsin than in any other place east of the Mississippi. When you come, we can walk around a model 17th century Ojibwa Village, see ancient burial mounds called "effigies" shaped like birds and animals, play lacrosse and listen to the music of Native American tribes at powwows. YAKAHAWE!

Jake

P.S. Boozhoo means "hello" in the Native Wisconsin Anishinaabemowen or Ojibwa language. Yakahawe is "so long for now" in the Oneida language.

On the twelfth day of Christmas, my cousin sent to me...

12 birch bark baskets

11 sundaes melting, 10 badgers snoozing, 9 snowmobilers, 8 cranes a-whooping, 7 planes a-swooping, 6 roadside giants, 5 golden rings, 4 pouncing pups, 3 huge fish, 2 roving Ducks, and a robin in a sugar maple tree.

Come back again soon!

Wisconsin: The Badger State

Capital: Madison • **State abbreviation:** WI • **Largest city:** Milwaukee • **State bird:** the robin
State flower: the wood violet • **State tree:** the sugar maple • **State animal:** the badger
State dog: the American Water Spaniel • **State motto:** "Forward"

Some Famous Wisconsinites:

Roy Chapman Andrews (1884-1960) was an explorer and naturalist born in Beloit. He led expeditions through China and Mongolia and found rare dinosaur fossils.

Harry Houdini (1874-1926), a famous magician and escape artist, lived in Appleton as a child.

James Arthur Lovell, Jr. (1928-), a NASA Astronaut, grew up in Milwaukee. He flew on four Gemini and Apollo space missions and was commander of the Apollo 13 mission to the moon.

John Muir (1838-1914) lived as a child in rural Marquette County. He became one of the first environmental conservationists, fighting to save America's wilderness areas and founding the Sierra Club.

Gaylord Nelson (1916-2005) was born in Clear Lake and grew up to be a U.S. Senator and Governor of Wisconsin. He founded Earth Day, first celebrated on April 22, 1970.

George Orson Welles (1915-1985), born in Kenosha, was a famous actor, broadcaster, and film director. His film *Citizen Kane* is a classic movie, considered by some to be the greatest film ever made.

Laura Ingalls Wilder (1867-1957), born in Pepin, was the author of the Little House series, including *Little House in the Big Woods* and *Little House on the Prairie,* based on her experiences growing up in a pioneer family.

Frank Lloyd Wright (1867-1959), a world-famous architect, was born in Richland Center. The buildings he designed include the Guggenheim Museum (NYC) and Fallingwater, a house in Pennsylvania. Taliesin, the home and studio he designed near Spring Green, is a National Historic Landmark.

STERLING and the distinctive Sterling logo are
registered trademarks of Sterling Publishing Co,. Inc

Library of Congress Cataloging-in-Publication Data
Kono, Erin Eitter.
The twelve days of Christmas in Wisconsin / Erin Eitter Kono.
p. cm.
ISBN-13: 978-1-4027-3815-9
ISBN-10: 1-4027-3815-3
1. Wisconsin—Juvenile literature. 2. Counting—Juvenile literature. I. Title.
F581.3.K66 2007
977.5—dc22
2007003950

10 9 8 7 6 5 4 3 2

Published by Sterling Publishing Co., Inc.
387 Park Avenue South, New York, NY 10016
© 2007 by Erin Eitter Kono
Distributed in Canada by Sterling Publishing
c/o Canadian Manda Group,
165 Dufferin Street, Toronto, Ontario, Canada M6K 3H6
Distributed in the United Kingdom by GMC Distribution Services
Castle Place, 166 High Street, Lewes, East Sussex, England BN7 1XU
Distributed in Australia by Capricorn Link (Australia) Pty. Ltd.
P.O. Box 704, Windsor, NSW 2756, Australia

Printed in China

Sterling ISBN 978-1-4027-3815-9

For information about custom editions, special sales, premium and
corporate purchases, please contact Sterling Special Sales Department
at 800-805-5489 or specialsales@sterlingpublishing.com.

The artwork was prepared using acrylic paint, pen, pencil
and digital collage on watercolor paper.

Acknowledgments
Many thanks to our superb researchers:
Margaret Woollatt, children's book editor and travel enthusiast,
and Sue-Marie Rendall, former Youth Services Librarian at
Portage County Public Library in Stevens Point, Wisconsin

To Caitlyn Akiko, who I like EVEN MORE than Wisconsin cheese!